W9-CPD-918

MOUSE
LOVES LOVE

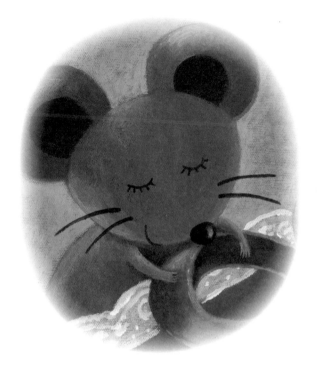

by Lauren Thompson
illustrated by Buket Erdogan

Ready-to-Read

Simon Spotlight

New York   London   Toronto   Sydney   New Delhi

SIMON SPOTLIGHT
An imprint of Simon & Schuster Children's Publishing Division
1230 Avenue of the Americas, New York, New York 10020
This Simon Spotlight edition December 2018
Text copyright © 2002, 2018 by Lauren Thompson
Illustrations copyright © 2002 by Buket Erdogan
Manufactured in the United States of America 1118 LAK
10 9 8 7 6 5 4 3 2 1
Library of Congress Cataloging-in-Publication Data
Names: Thompson, Lauren, 1962– author. | Erdogan, Buket, illustrator.
Title: Mouse loves love / by Lauren Thompson ; illustrated by Buket Erdogan.
Description: New York, NY : Simon Spotlight, 2018. | Series: Ready-to-Read | Series: Mouse | Summary: Mouse watches his sister, Minka, gather a collection of craft items and then put them together to make something special. | Identifiers: LCCN 2018030112 (print) | LCCN 2018035897 (eBook) | ISBN 9781534421516 (eBook) | ISBN 9781534421493 (paperback) | ISBN 9781534421509 (hardcover) | Subjects: | CYAC: Valentines—Fiction. | Valentine's Day—Fiction. | Brothers and sisters—Fiction. | Mice—Fiction. | BISAC: JUVENILE FICTION / Readers / Beginner. | JUVENILE FICTION / Animals / Mice, Hamsters, Guinea Pigs, etc. | JUVENILE FICTION / Imagination & Play. | Classification: LCC PZ7.T37163 (eBook) | LCC PZ7.T37163 Mu 2018 (print) | DDC [E]—dc23
LC record available at https://lccn.loc.gov/2018030112

The illustrations and portions of the text were previously published in 2002 in *Mouse's First Valentine*.

One day,
big sister Minka
sneaks away.

Mouse sneaks away too!

Where is Minka going?

Minka creeps
high and low
and all around.

She finds something smooth and rosy.
What is it?

"Red paper!" says Minka.

"Just what I need."

Next Minka races
over and under
and all around.

She finds something
white and holey.
What is it?

"Lace!" says Minka.

"Just what I need."

Then Minka leaps
here and there
and all around.

She finds something
shiny and curly.
What is it?

"Ribbon!" says Minka.

"Just what I need."

Next Minka peeks
inside and outside
and all around.

She finds something
sticky and goopy.
What is it?

"Paste!" says Minka.

"Just what I need."

Now Minka folds the
paper like this.

What is Minka making?

Then Minka brushes the
paste like that.

What could it be?

Next Minka smooths
the lace like this.

What is it?

Then Minka ties the
ribbon like that.

What can Minka be making?

At last Minka says,

"It's ready!"

"Come here, little Mouse!"
says Minka.

"This valentine is just for **you**! Just because . . .

"I love you!"